THE PRINCESS AND THE WARRIOR

A Tale of Two Volcanoes

DUNCAN TONATIUH

ABRAMS BOOKS FOR YOUNG READERS · NEW YORK

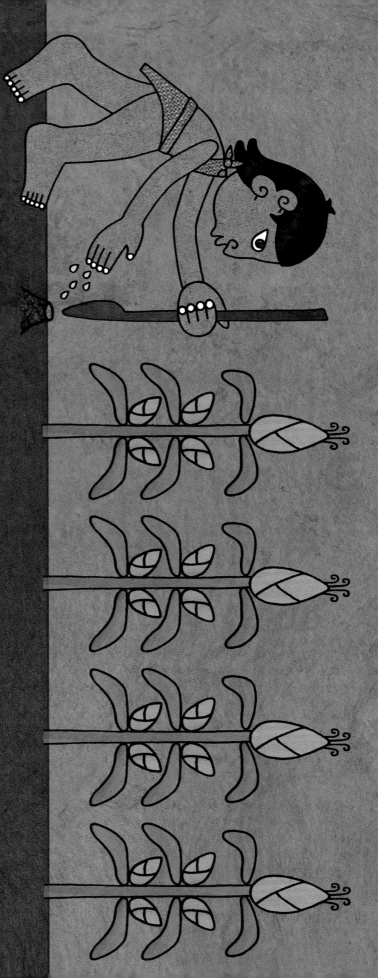

nce upon a time, there lived a kind and beautiful princess named Izta. Even though she was the daughter of an emperor, she loved to spend time with the people who grew corn in the *milpas*. She liked to teach them poetry, or *flor y canto*.

Suitors traveled from distant lands to woo her. They presented her with rare and lavish gifts, such as quetzal feathers and turquoise necklaces.

They would all say the same thing. "You are the most beautiful maiden in the land! Marry me, princess, and you will live in my luxurious palace. You won't have to spend time in the fields ever again."

"No, thank you," Izta would reply. She was not interested in any of the suitors or their gifts.

One day, a warrior named Popoca came to see her. "Princess, I know you have a kind and beautiful heart, for I have seen you teaching *flor y canto* to the villagers in the *milpas*. I don't have expensive gifts to offer, but if you marry me, I promise that I will love you for who you are. I will stay by your side no matter what, as long as *tonatiuh* rises, as long as the *cenzontle* bird sings."

6

Popoca's words were music to Izta's ears. She could hear the honesty in his voice, and she fell in love with him.

The emperor did not want his daughter to marry a mere soldier. He wanted her to marry a wealthy and powerful *tlatoani*, a ruler. But he knew that Popoca was the best and bravest warrior in his kingdom. The emperor and his people had been at war with Jaguar Claw, the *tlatoani* of a neighboring land, for years, and there seemed to be no end in sight. He called Popoca to him.

"Popoca," the emperor said, "if you defeat Jaguar Claw once and for all, I will let you marry my daughter, Izta."

Popoca and Izta were overjoyed! Popoca gathered his most courageous men and marched to war.

9

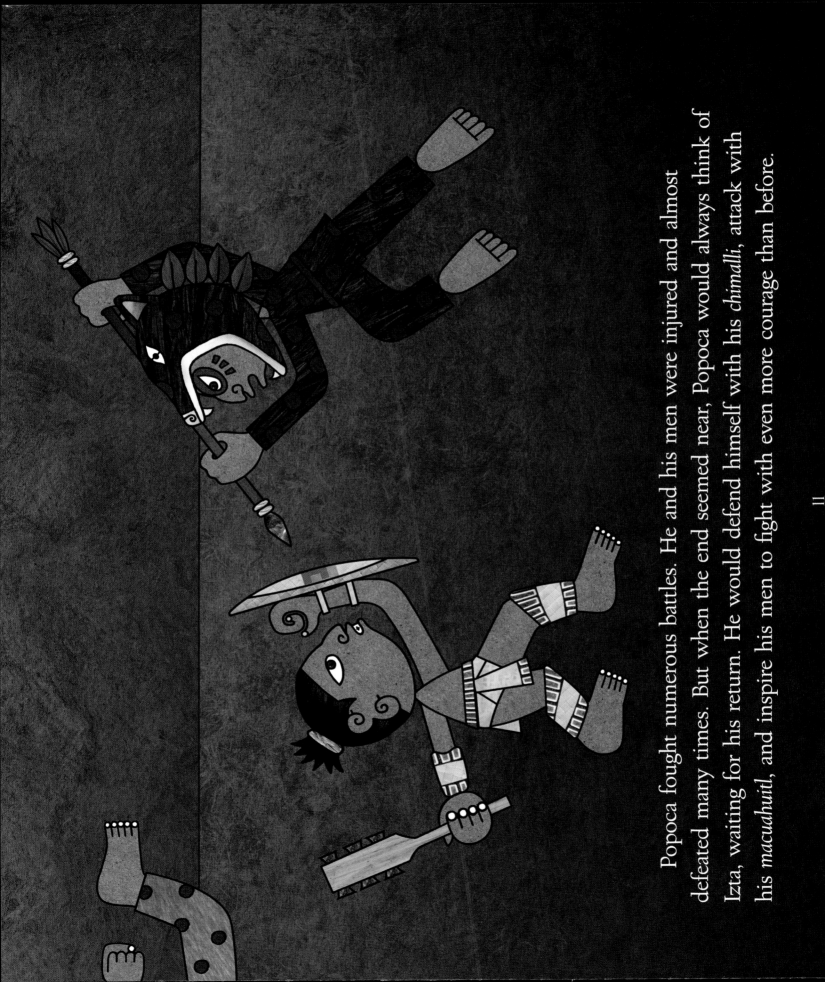

Popoca fought numerous battles. He and his men were injured and almost defeated many times. But when the end seemed near, Popoca would always think of Izta, waiting for his return. He would defend himself with his *chimalli*, attack with his *macuahuitl*, and inspire his men to fight with even more courage than before.

Slowly, the tide turned, and Popoca and his men began winning battles. It was clear that they would soon defeat Jaguar Claw.

Realizing this, Jaguar Claw devised a plan to steal from Popoca what the warrior cherished most. He bribed one of Popoca's personal messengers. "Tell Izta that Popoca has been killed, and offer her this potion, *octli*, to soothe her grief."

14

"Everything is lost, princess," the messenger said sadly when he arrived at the palace. "Popoca and his men fought bravely, but they were defeated and killed."

"No! That cannot be!" cried Izta. She locked herself in her chamber and wept, and refused to eat or speak with anyone.

That night, the messenger came to her room. "I know your heart is shattered as if it were made of obsidian glass," he said. "But take this drink, princess. It will help ease your grief."

Izta took the potion and drank it all. Lying down on her *petlatl*, she fell into a deep sleep.

The next day, before night fell and the first *citlalli* appeared in the sky, Popoca defeated Jaguar Claw. Unaware of the lies the messenger had told, the great warrior and his troops marched back to the palace in triumph, ready to share the good news with the princess and the emperor.

But when they arrived, they were met with disbelief. "Popoca!" said the emperor. "One of your messengers told us that you were dead! Izta was heartbroken. She took a special *octli* to ease her pain, and now we cannot wake her."

"This can't be true!" said Popoca. "Izta, my beautiful princess, has to awaken!" He ran to her chamber. He kissed her and held her in his arms. He called out her name, over and over.

But Izta did not wake up.

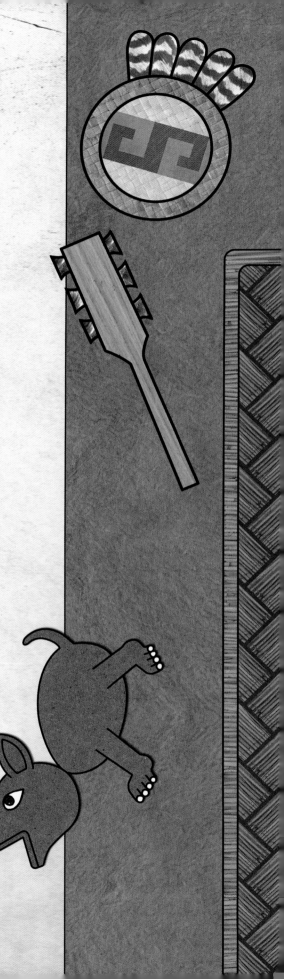

"Cool air will surely revive her," Popoca told the emperor. He carried Izta through the throngs of villagers, who wept as they passed, past the *milpas*, and all through the night to the top of a *tépetl*.

22

He laid her on a *xóchitl* bed.

He knelt down beside her.

The cool mountain air soon turned to snow. But still the princess did not wake up.

Popoca refused to move. He stayed next to Izta, just as he had promised when he first met her. As long as *tonatiuh* rises, as long as the *cenzontle* bird sings.

26

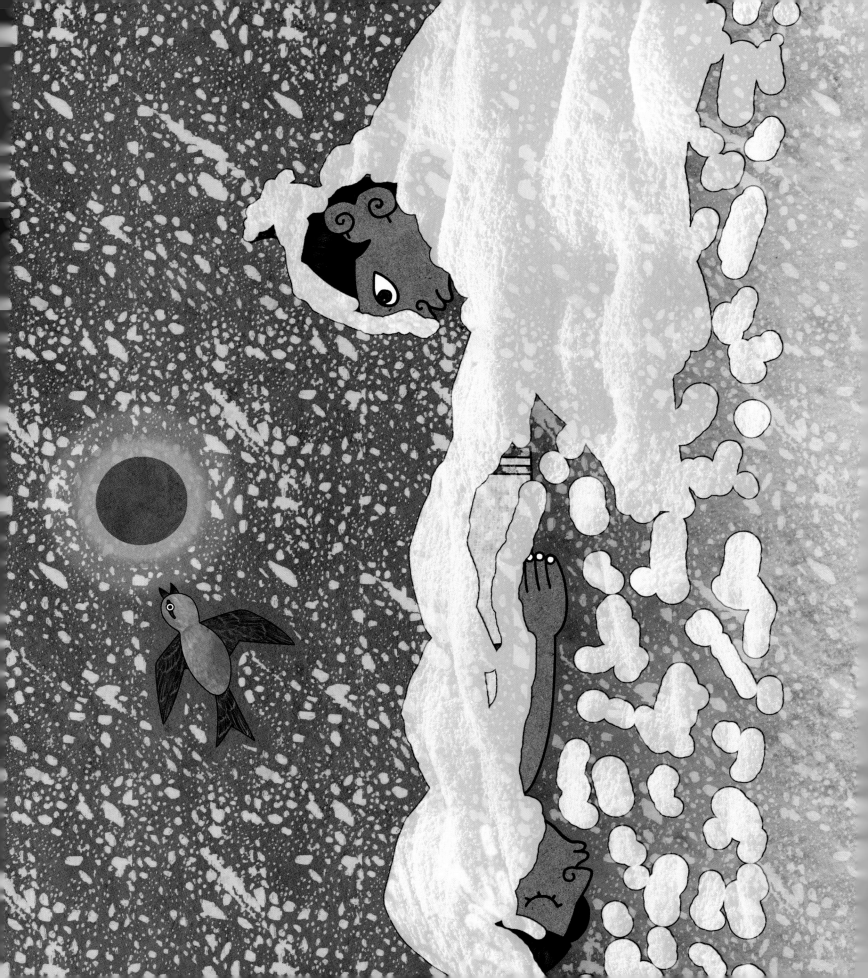

In time, where once there was a princess with her true love by her side, two volcanoes emerged. One is known as Iztaccíhuatl, or sleeping woman. The other one is known as Popocatépetl, or smoky mountain. Iztaccíhuatl continues to sleep. But Popocatépetl spews ashes and smoke from time to time, as if attempting to wake his sleeping princess.

AUTHOR'S NOTE

ztaccihuatl [ease-tah-SEE-what-tl] and Popocatépetl [poh-poh-kah-TEH-peh-tl] are two volcanoes located approximately forty miles southeast of Mexico City, a city that hundreds of years ago used to be the Aztec city of Tenochtitlán (teh-nosh-tee-TLAN). Iztaccíhuatl is dormant, but Popocatépetl is an active volcano. Its most recent eruption occurred in 2013, when it spewed ashes and fragments of fiery rock. Iztaccíhuatl, the third highest volcano in Mexico, is 17,160 feet tall. Popocatépetl is 17,802 feet tall and is the second highest volcano in Mexico and the fifth highest in North America.

The name Iztaccíhuatl comes from the Nahuatl language. *Iztac* means white, and *cihuatl* means woman. The volcano is often called the Sleeping Woman, *la Mujer Dormida*, because the four peaks that form the volcano resemble the silhouette of a woman lying down, draped in a blanket of white snow. The name Popocatépetl comes from the Nahuatl words *popoca*, smoking, and *tépetl*, mountain. The volcano is often called el Popo for short and sometimes Don Goyo—Mr. Gregory—by the villagers of the region.

These two majestic volcanoes can be seen on most days by millions of people who live in Mexico City, one of the largest metropolitan areas in the world. Hundreds of years ago, the volcanoes could be seen by the Aztecs, the Tlaxcalans, and the different peoples who lived in the central valley of Mexico. The beauty and the imposing presence of the volcanoes have inspired several stories. The most famous story by far is the legend of their origin.

The author of the legend is unknown. The story has been passed down orally from generation to generation for centuries. There are different variations of the story. In some versions, Popoca is an Aztec warrior who is sent to war—sometimes to Oaxaca, sometimes to Tlaxcala—while his beloved princess awaits him. In other versions, he is a Tlaxcalan warrior rebelling against the mighty Aztec empire. But in all the versions, Popoca returns from war and watches ceaselessly over his beloved princess until the two of them transform into volcanoes.

The story I tell in this book is my own version. I have included some of my own twists and details. For instance, I chose to name Popoca's enemy Jaguar Claw because there was a famous Mixtec warrior king in the eleventh century named Eight Deer Jaguar Claw who appears in several ancient codices, like the Codex Colombino, the Codex Zouche-Nuttall, and the Codex Bodley. My illustrations draw from the images in those Mixtec codices, and I wanted to pay tribute to them. Readers may notice how in my drawings, as in the ones from those codices, people and animals are always drawn in profile. Their entire bodies are usually shown, and their ears often look like the number 3.

Iztaccíhuatl and Popocatépetl have inspired artists for hundreds, perhaps even thousands, of years. Storytellers, poets, painters, photographers, and others have created pieces of art to honor the magnificent mountains. My hope is that my story contributes to this vast tradition of art, and that it introduces the volcanoes and their legend to a new generation of young readers.

GLOSSARY

I have included some foreign words in the book, but rather than using Spanish, I used Nahuatl, since that's the language Popoca and Izta would have spoken. Many words of Nahuatl origin have become part of Spanish as it is spoken nowadays.

cenzontle [sen-SON-tleh]: mockingbird. In Nahuatl, the word *cenzontle* means "bird with a hundred voices." *Cenzontles* have an impressive ability to mimic other sounds, especially other bird songs. *Cenzontles* can be found throughout North America, Central America, and the Caribbean.

chimalli [CHEE-mah-lee]: shield.

citlalli [see-tla-LEE]: star. It is sometimes used as a first name or middle name.

flor y canto [floor ee KHAN-toh]: flower and song. It is the name that the people of the central valley of Mexico gave to poetry before the Spanish conquest.

macuahuitl [MAH-qua-we-tl]: a wooden sword covered with very sharp obsidian blades. The weapon was common among various Mesoamerican civilizations.

milpas [MEEL-pahs]: a word that can be translated as "fields." *Milpas* are a system of growing crops that dates back to pre-Columbian times. The system usually involves growing corn, beans, and squash simultaneously.

obsidian: a type of glass that's produced when volcanic magma cools rapidly. Obsidian was used by many Mesoamerican civilizations to create sharp tools and weapons.

octli [OC-tlee]: a fermented beverage made from the sap of the maguey, a type of agave plant. *Octli* was drunk in pre-Columbian times for ceremonial and religious purposes. The alcoholic drink continues to be consumed nowadays throughout Mexico and is commonly known as *pulque.*

petlatl [peh-TLA-tl] or **petate** [peh-TAH-teh]: a mat woven from the fibers of a small palm. In pre-Columbian times, *petlatls* were used as bedrolls. They continue to be used today for sleeping and for other purposes.

quetzal [KET-sal]: a type of bird with bright green feathers that can be found in the south of Mexico and in Central America.

tépetl [TEH-peh-tl]: mountain.

tlatoani [tlah-toh-AN-ee]: ruler or king.

tonatiuh [TOH-nah-tee-oo]: sun or sun god. In Aztec mythology there are five sun gods and eras. We are currently in the era of the fifth sun, Ollin Tonatiuh. It is sometimes used as a first name or middle name.

turquoise: a blue and green stone that was of great value to the Aztecs and other Mesoamerican cultures.

xóchitl [SAW-chee-tl]: flower. It is sometimes used as a first name or middle name.

BIBLIOGRAPHY

Anawait, Patricia Rieff. *Indian Clothing Before Cortés: Mesoamerican Costumes from the Codices*. Norman, Oklahoma: University of Oklahoma Press, 1981.

Chambers, Bradford. *Aztecs of Mexico: The Lost Civilization*. New York: Grosset & Dunlap, 1965.

Los dos volcanes. Popocatépetl e Iztaccíhuatl. Artes de México #73, 2005.

Iturbe, Mercedes, ed. *El mito de dos volcanes: Popocatépetl, Iztaccíhuatl*. Mexico City: Instituto Nacional de Bellas Artes y Literatura: Editorial RM, 2005.

Jordan, Philip D. *The Burro Benedicto and Other Folktales and Legends of Mexico*. New York: McCann, 1960.

Martínez, Susana. *Leyendas de los antiguos mexicanos*. Mexico City: Editores Mexicanos Unidos, 2003.

Melgar, Juan Carlos. *Xochiquetzal y Popoca. La leyenda de los volcanes*. Mexico City: Cacciani, 2015.

Von Hagen, Victor W. *The Sun Kingdom of the Aztecs*. Cleveland: World Publishing, 1958.

aulex.org/nah-es/ [Spanish-Nahuat dictionary]

whp.uoregon.edu/dictionaries/nahuatl/ [English-Nahuatl dictionary]

THE ART IN THIS BOOK WAS HAND-DRAWN, THEN COLLAGED DIGITALLY.

Cataloging-in-Publication Data has been applied for and may be obtained from the Library of Congress.

ISBN: 978-1-4197-2130-4

Text and illustrations copyright © 2016 Duncan Tonatiuh
Book design by Maria T. Middleton

Printed and bound in China

10 9 8 7 6 5 4 3 2 1

Abrams Books for Young Readers are available at special discounts when purchased in quantity for premiums and promotions as well as fundraising or educational use. Special editions can also be created to specification. For details, contact specialsales@abramsbooks.com or the address below.

ABRAMS
THE ART OF BOOKS SINCE 1949
115 West 18th Street
New York, NY 10011
www.abramsbooks.com

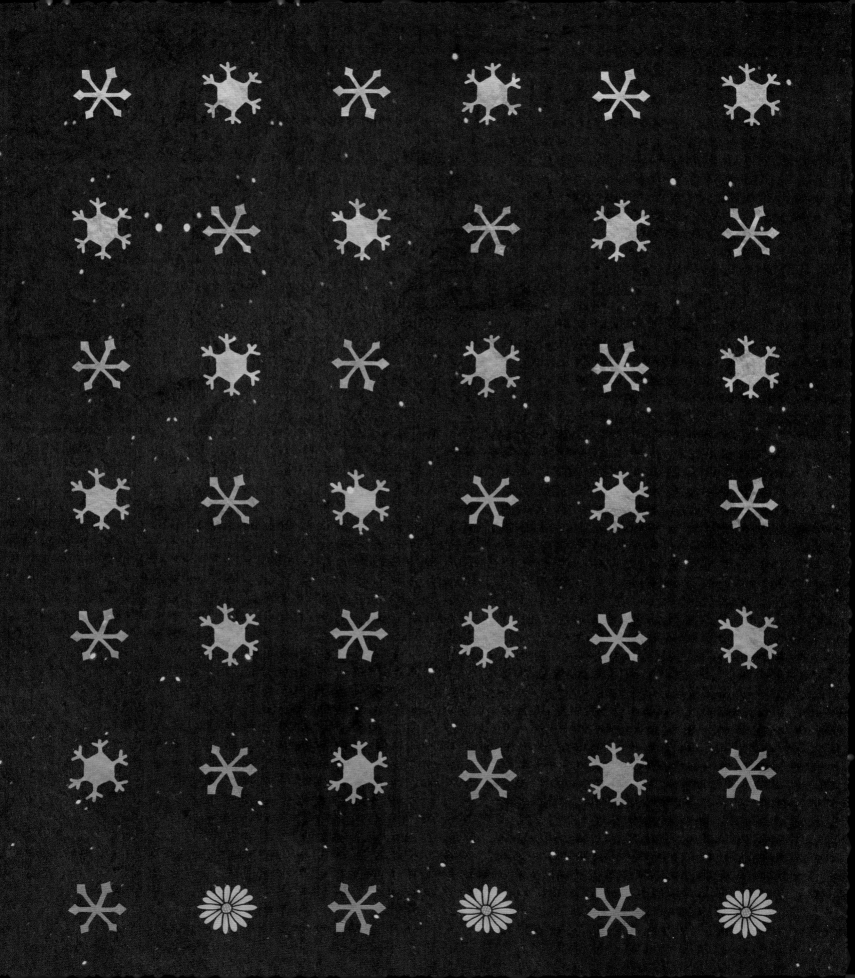